Disney · PIXAR

FRIENDS TO THE FINISH

Adapted by Natasha Bouchard

Illustrated by the Disney Storybook Artists

A GOLDEN BOOK ● NEW YORK

Materials and characters from the movie *Cars 2*. Copyright © 2011 Disney/Pixar. Disney/Pixar elements © Disney/Pixar, not including underlying vehicles owned by third parties; and, if applicable: Pacer and Gremlin are trademarks of Chrysler LLC; Jeep® and the Jeep® grille design are registered trademarks of Chrysler LLC; Mercury is a registered trademark of Ford Motor Company; Porsche is a trademark of Porsche; Sarge's rank insignia design used with the approval of the U.S. Army; Volkswagen trademarks, design patents and copyrights are used with the approval of the owner, Volkswagen AG; Bentley is a trademark of Bentley Motors Limited; FIAT and Topolino are trademarks of FIAT S.p.A.; Monte Carlo, Corvette, El Dorado, and Chevrolet Impala are trademarks of General Motors. Background inspired by the Cadillac Ranch by Ant Farm (Lord, Michels and Marquez) © 1974. All rights reserved. Published in the United States by Golden Books, an imprint of Random House Children's Books, a division of Random House, Inc., 1745 Broadway, New York, NY 10019, and in Canada by Random House of Canada Limited, Toronto, in conjunction with Disney Enterprises, Inc. Golden Books, A Golden Book, and the G colophon are registered trademarks of Random House, Inc.

ISBN: 978-0-7364-2805-7

www.randomhouse.com/kids

Printed in the United States of America

10 9 8 7 6 5 4 3 2

Far from Radiator Springs, a secret agent is hard at work.

England's top-secret agent uncovers an evil plan.
Use the key to decode his name.

I   N   F   M   R

F i n n

ANSWER: Finn.

Uh-oh! The bad guys spot Agent Finn!
Solve the maze to help Finn escape.

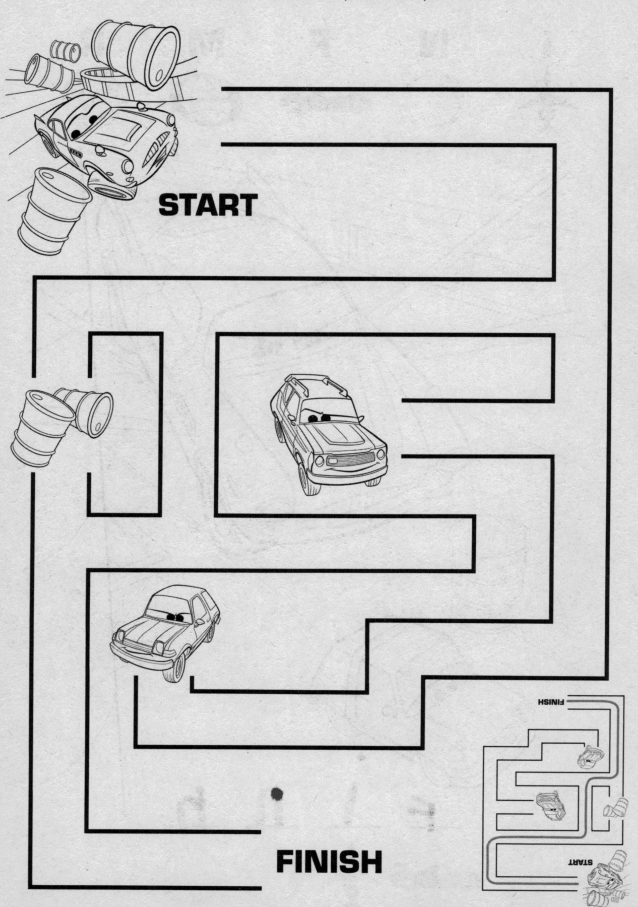

START

FINISH

FINISH

START

ANSWER:

Mater is a tow truck. He is Lightning McQueen's best friend.

Everyone is busy in Radiator Springs.
No one has time for Mater . . . not even Lightning.

Lightning likes spending time with Sally.

Mater calls in to the Mel Dorado television show.

Lightning and Mater head off to the first race of the World Grand Prix!

Fillmore and Sarge are part of Team Lightning. Look at the top picture carefully.
Then circle 5 things that are different in the bottom picture.

ANSWER:

In Japan, Lightning gears up for the first race.

There is so much to see in Tokyo! Lightning watches a sumo-wrestling match.

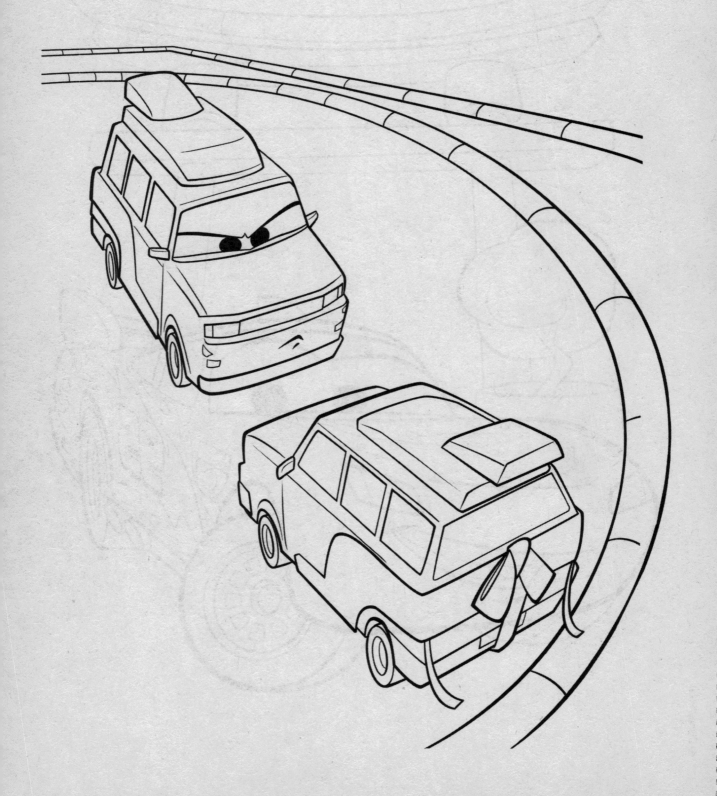

Kabuki cars perform in the theater.

Team Lightning spends the night in a cube hotel.

Mater can't believe his eyes! Tires . . . from a vending machine!

Mater and Lightning even visit a store that sells Lightning McQueen toys!

Lightning is excited to meet Miles Axlerod, a famous electric car.

Miles Axlerod created a special fuel for race cars. To find out the name of this new fuel, follow the lines and write each letter on the correct blank.

N L O L A L I

— — — — — — — —

Finn McMissile is looking for an American agent with secret information.

Holley Shiftwell is another secret agent. She works with Finn.

It's a spy search! Circle the 5 objects
that don't belong in this picture.

ANSWER:

Mater is confused by the foreign machines in the bathroom.

Torque, the American secret agent, hides a special device on Mater.

Grem and Acer are Lemons—cars that break down a lot. They want
the device Torque had . . . so now they're after Mater!

Holley thinks Mater is the American secret agent.

Finn also thinks Mater is the American agent.

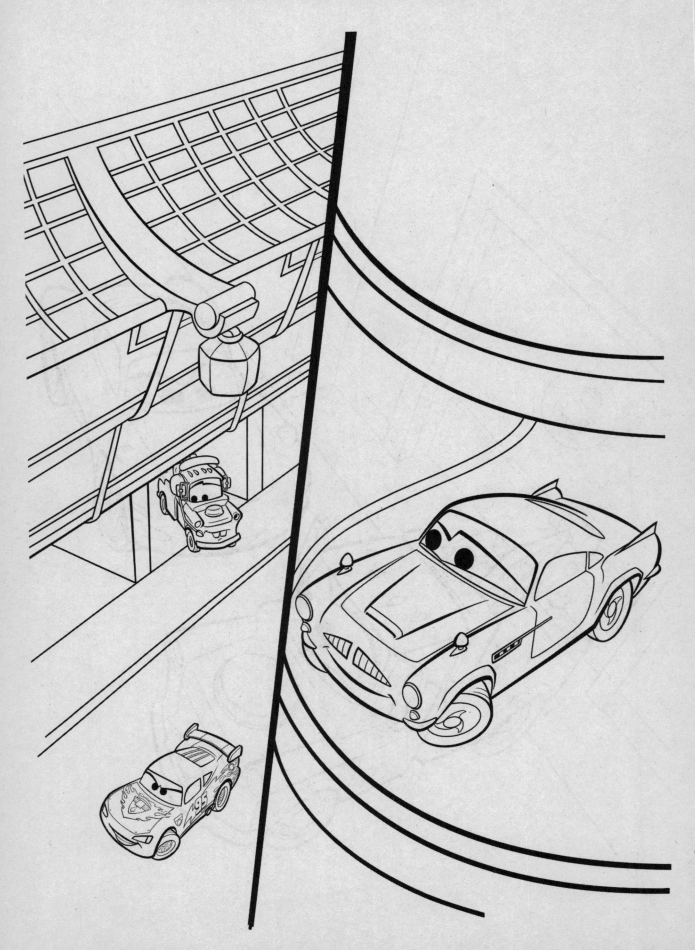

The evil scientist thinks Torque is hiding the device.

Who is this evil scientist? To find out, cross out every *T*.
Then write the remaining letters in order on the blanks.

T P T R T O T F T T E
T S T S T O T R T T Z

— — — — — — — — —

Lightning's team is all set for the first World Grand Prix race.

A race car's engine blows up during the race!

Grem and Acer are up to something suspicious.

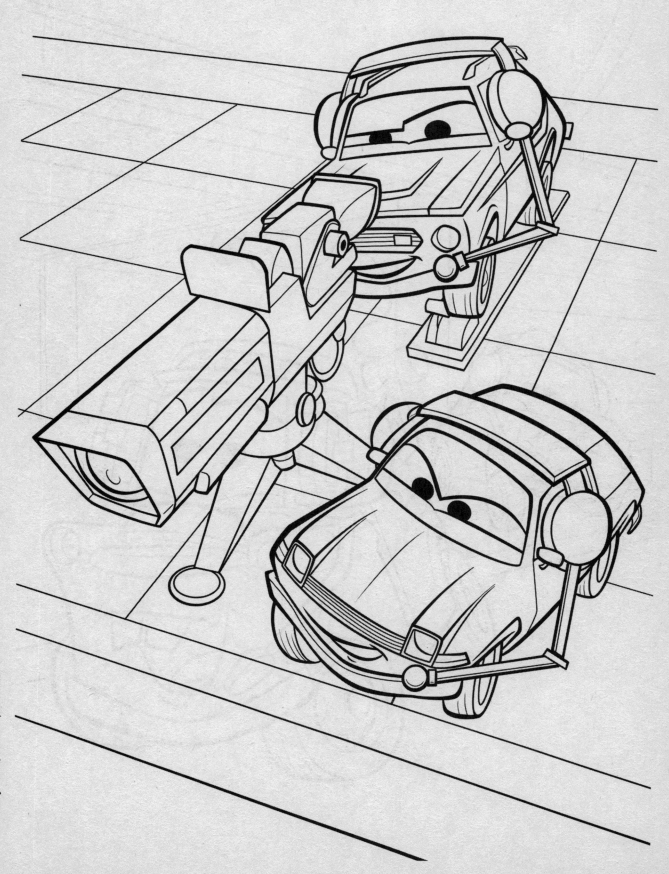

Mater hears a voice in his headset. It's Holley!

Mater's conversation with Holley causes Lightning
to swerve all over the racetrack!

Lightning loses the first World Grand Prix race.

What is the name of the racer who wins? To find out, replace each
letter with the one that comes before it in the alphabet.

G S B O D F T D P

___ ___ ___ ___ ___ ___ ___ ___ ___

ANSWER: Francesco.

Lightning is upset with Mater for making him lose the race.

Using his special karate moves, Finn stops Grem from capturing Mater.

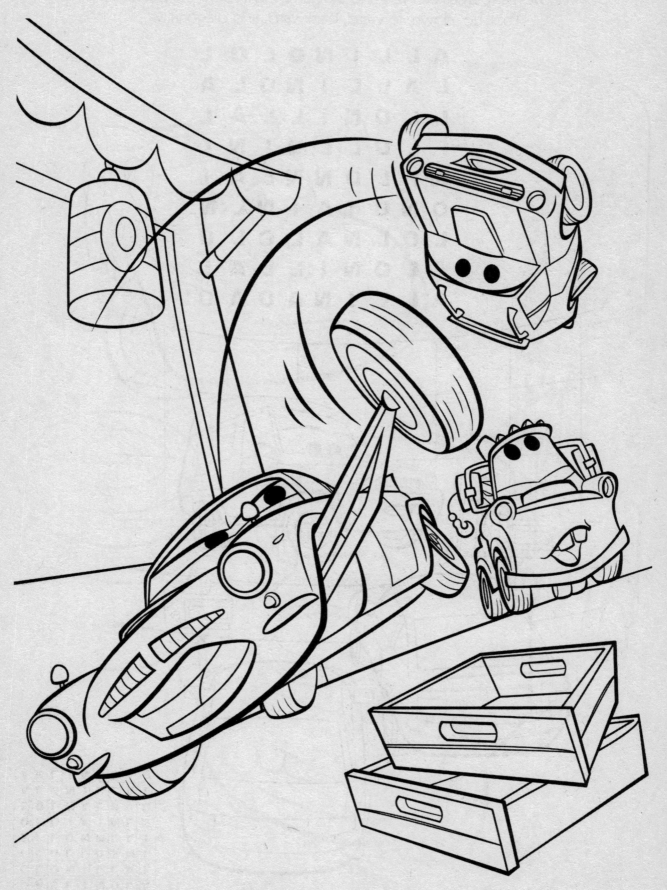

The press blames the fuel Allinol for the exploding engines.
How many times can you find the name ALLINOL in the puzzle?
Look up, down, forward, backward, and diagonally.

```
A L L I N O L O L
L A L L I N O L A
L L O N I L L A L
I L O L L O I N L
N I L O N N L A I
O N O I A I N L N
L O L N A L O L O
A L O N I L L A L
A L L I N A O A O
```

Mater thinks he made Lightning lose the race.

Wearing a disguise, Finn follows Mater to the airport.

Grem and Acer try to catch Mater before he gets on the plane.

Finn helps keep Mater busy, and away from the Lemons.

Siddeley is a spy plane.

Help Finn and Mater reach Holley before Grem and Acer catch them.

START

FINISH

ANSWER:

Acer ends up in a truck full of sewage.

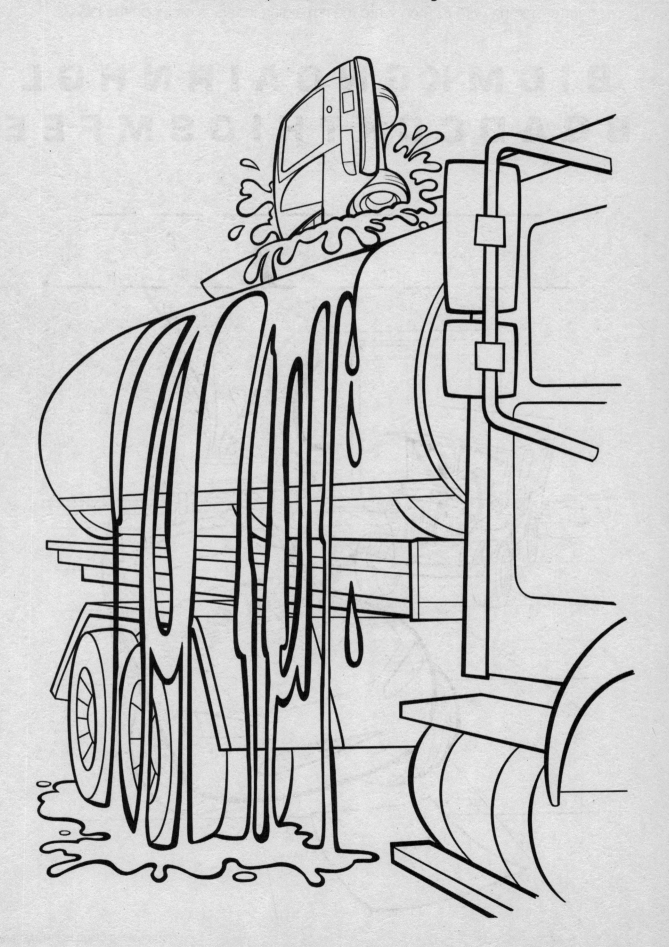

Lightning finds a note from Mater. What does it say? To find out, cross out every other letter starting with B. Then write the remaining letters in order on the blanks.

B I C M K G N O A I R N H G L
B Q A D C C K T H I O S M F E E

__ , __ __ __ __ __ __ __

__ __ __ __ __ __ __ .

ANSWER: I'm going back home.

Guido and Luigi miss Mater.

Mater uncovers a clue!

Thanks to Mater, Finn and Holley come up with a plan!

Where do Mater, Finn, and Holley fly next to uncover more clues?
Unscramble the letters to find out.

ASIPR

— — — — —

Mater and Finn follow Tomber, a French car-parts dealer, to a private location.

Tomber tells Holley and Finn about a secret meeting.

Team Lightning arrives in Italy for the second
World Grand Prix race and meets Uncle Topolino.

Guido and Luigi are happy to be back in their hometown.

Luigi's Uncle Topolino is very wise.

Lightning tells Uncle Topolino that he misses Mater.

Circle the two pictures of Guido and Luigi that are exactly the same.

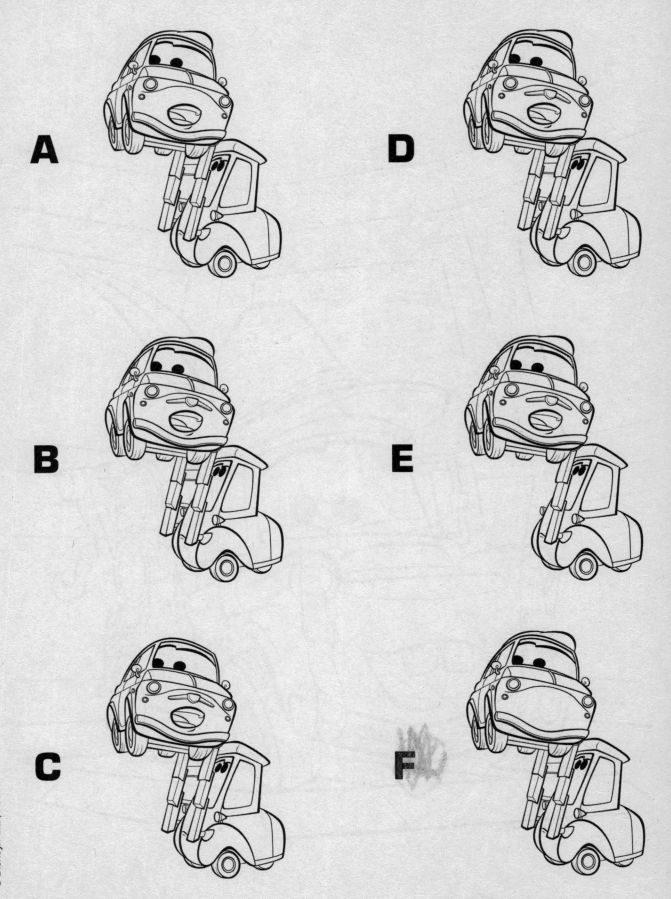

A

B

C

D

E

F

ANSWER: B and D.

Secret agent Mater is ready to go undercover!

Mater's in disguise! Find 5 differences between
the two pictures of Mater below.

ANSWER:

Francesco is sure he will win the second race, too.

Francesco adores all the attention he gets from his fans.

While wearing a disguise, Mater overhears Grem and Acer
talking about their camera, which is causing the race cars to crash!

Carla Veloso is Brazil's superstar race car!

Jeff Gorvette is an American race car.

The second race begins!

Lightning wants to prove that he is faster than Francesco.

Lightning wins the second race of the World Grand Prix!

Circle the picture of Max Schnell and Miguel Camino
that is different from the others.

1

2

3

4

5

Flo, Sally, and Red join Team Lightning for the next race.

Sally is always ready to help her friends.

Finn gets snagged by the Lemons!

Armed with rockets and a parachute, Mater rushes to save Lightning!

Oh, no! Mater has been captured!

Holley and Mater are held captive in Big Bentley!
How will they stop the race?

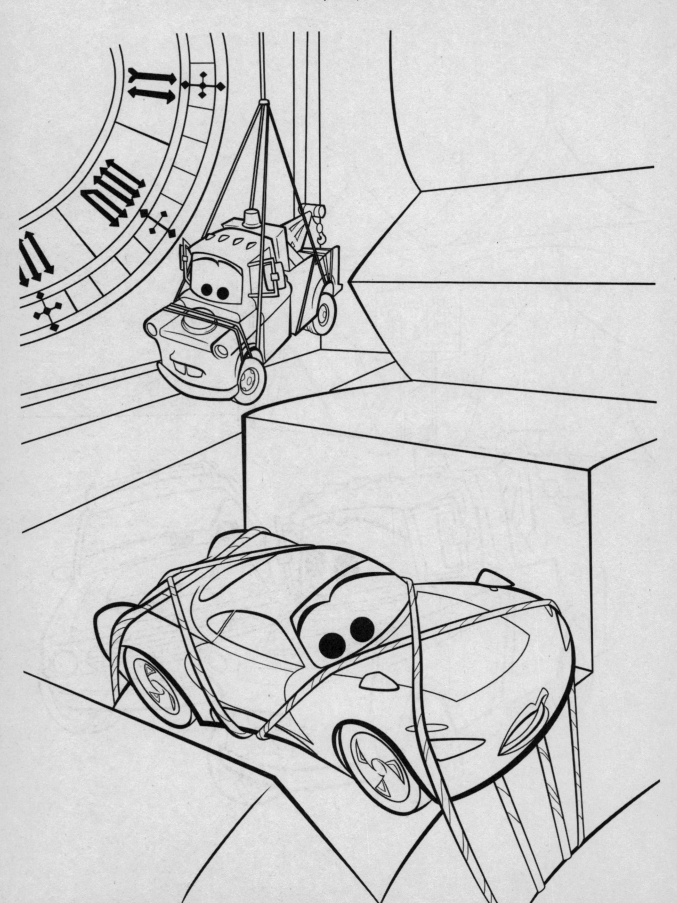

Is this the end of Mater?

Holley uses her wings to break out of Big Bentley!

Help Mater stop Lightning from competing in the London race!
Find the line that leads Mater to Lightning.

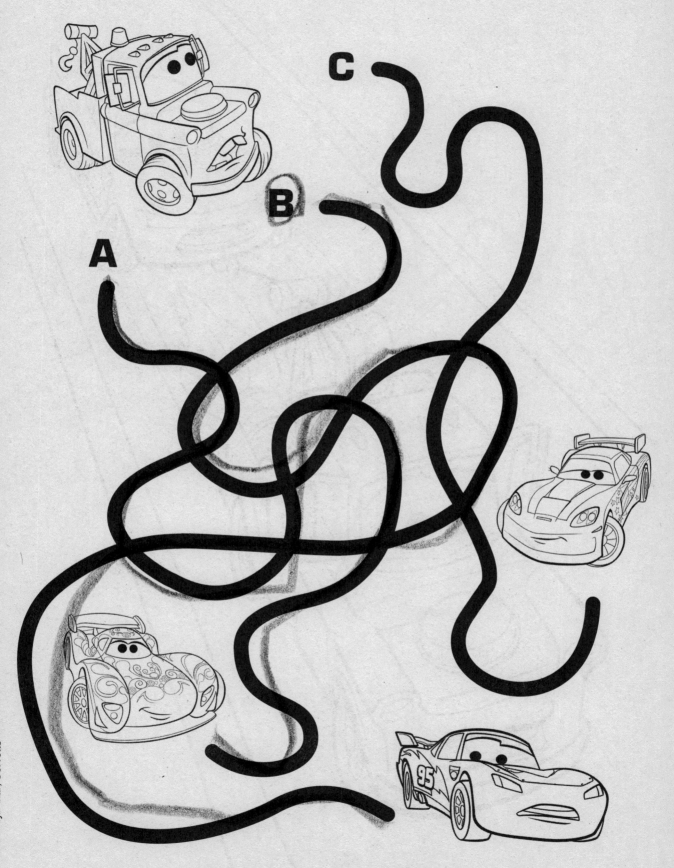

C

B

A

ANSWER: B.

Mater rockets to the rescue!

Use the key to color Mater.

1 = YELLOW 2 = ORANGE 3 = BROWN 4 = RED

Holley swoops in on Acer.

Holley sends Grem and Acer flying.

Finn hooks on to Professor Z!

Ramone spray-paints one of the bad guys!

Red is ready for action!

Guido uses some quick moves to slow down this Lemon!

Only Lightning and Mater can save the day!

Who does Mater meet? Use the key to find out.

Mater tells the Queen about the evil plot against the race cars!

Mater explains how Allinol and the race camera
were causing the race cars to crash.

Lightning and Mater are relieved. Everyone is safe.

The Queen thanks Mater for solving the mystery by making him a knight.

Lightning and Mater welcome the racers to Radiator Springs.

Lightning and his rival, Francesco, are now friends.

Lightning and Francesco zoom around the track in a friendly race.

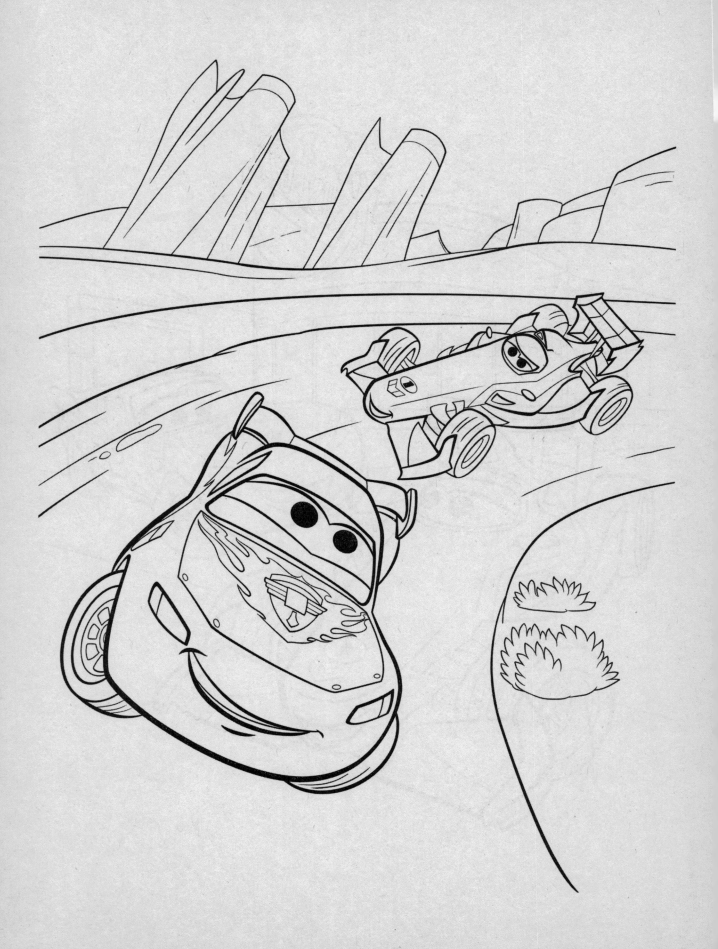

Finn and Holley want Mater to become a real secret agent.

Mater stays in Radiator Springs with his best friend, Lightning!